Who Is ANA DALT?

Written by
B.D. Cottleston

Illustrated by
Marcin Piwowarski

Why are some things just for Ana Dalt?

Who is Ana Dalt?

Why is she such a big deal?

I'm hoping one day to tell her how I feel.

I'd say, "Hey, Ana Dalt! What about me?

Why can't I touch all the things that I see?

So many fun things seem to be just for you!

But I think you should share! I like those things, too!"

When I go to the store
and I see something cool,
like a riding lawn mower
or a gardening tool,
I start walking toward it,
and that's when they say...

"That's for ANA DALT!
The kids' aisle is that way!"

When I see something fragile, I want it so much!

But when I reach up to get it, someone always yells...

"DON'T TOUCH!"

"Only ANA DALT should be touching that stuff."
But all I am thinking is I've heard that enough!

When we're watching TV and a scary movie is starting,

you can be pretty sure that's the time I'm departing.

"This is for Ana Dalt!" is what's always said.

And SURPRISE, SURPRISE,

it's time I went to bed.

When I'm at a party and the food looks delicious,
the grown-ups watch me like I'm acting suspicious.
If I try to grab snacks that look good to eat,
they just take the food back and say...

"THAT'S NOT YOUR TREAT!"
"That's for Ana Dalt.

You should eat the kids' food."

But food just for you, Ana?

I think that's just rude!

Ana Dalt this! Ana Dalt that!

It's time someone tells me where Ana Dalt's at!

Has anyone told her it´s nicer to share?

Does she even know? Does she even care?

I'm frustrated and really think it's all her fault.
But I've looked everywhere and can't find Ana Dalt!

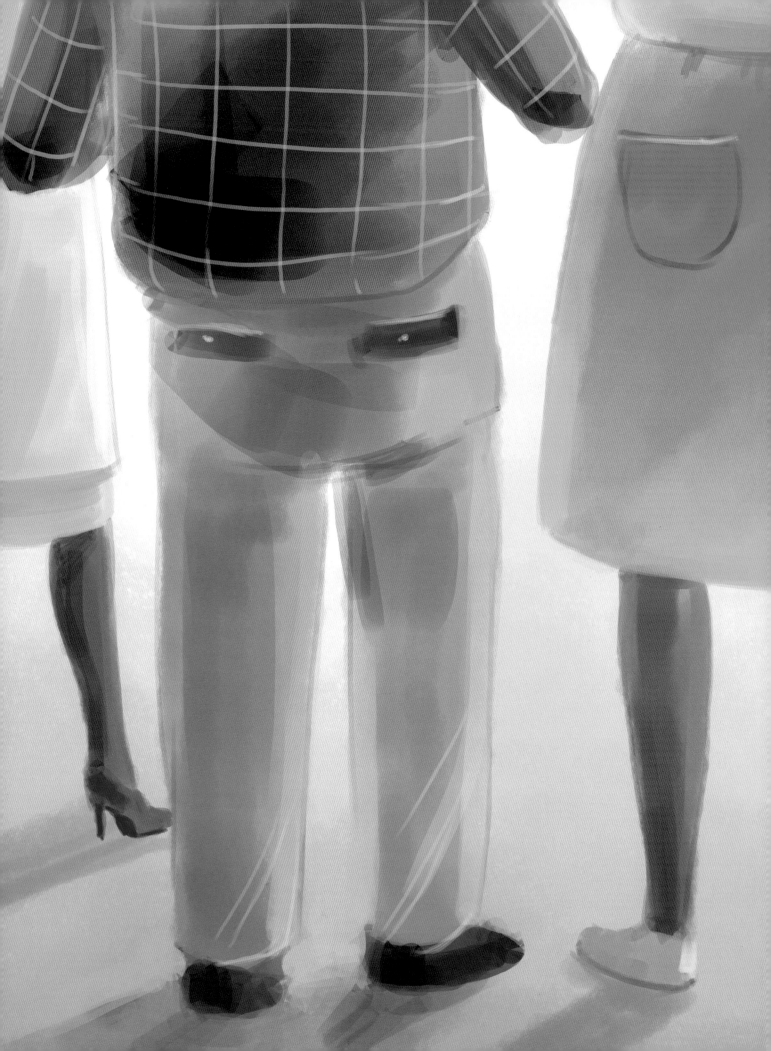

We could just ask the parents
if they know where she's staying,
since "ask Ana Dalt"
is what they keep saying.

Otherwise, I guess we will just never know
why Ana Dalt gets to keep running the show!